Love's GPS

Love's GPS

SILMA QUIÑONES

Primix Publishing
East Brunswick Office Evolution
1 Tower Center Boulevard, Ste 1510
East Brunswick, NJ 08816
www.primixpublishing.com
Phone: 1-800-538-5788

Published by Primix Publishing: 02/12/2025

ISBN: 979-8-89194-416-9(sc)
ISBN: 979-8-89194-417-6(e)

Library of Congress Control Number: Pending

Contents

Introduction vii

Chapter 1. How to Know if You Are Ready for a Romantic
Relationship 1
Questionnaires 8
My Family and Friends. 8
Profile of My Romantic Relationships. 9
Attributes of My Partners 11
Summary of My Relationships 11

Chapter 2. A Guide for Analyzing the Questionnaires 14
The Family Constellation 15
Like Father, Like Son 17
Family is Inherited; Friends are Chosen. 18
Your Enemies Say a Lot About You 19
Look at Yourself in the Same Mirror 19
In Summary... 20

Chapter 3. Selection Criteria. 21
Is the Person Available? 21
Lessons from Past Relationships 22
Love at First Sight: the Initial Attraction 24

Chapter 4. Personality Traits of Your Date 31
       Intelligence 33
       Age 34
       Responsibility 36
       Honesty .38
       Integrity .38
       Discipline 39
       Empathy 40
       Consideration for Others 41
       Passivity and Initiative 43
       Sociability 44

Chapter 5. Sexuality 45
       Gender 45
       Common Complaints About Sexuality: 50
       Haste and Impulsiveness 50
       Rigidity and Lack of Flexibility 51
       Shyness .52
       Aggressiveness 53
       Indifference 54
       The Machismo Attitude 55
       The Lack of Creativity 56
       Consideration in Sexual Intimacy 56

Chapter 6. Where to Find a Partner 58

Chapter 7. How to Evaluate a Potential Partner 61

Chapter 8. How to Know if You Are in Love and If It's Mutual . .65
       Defining Love 65
       Understanding Commitment 66

Introduction

Did you make a mistake by falling madly in love, only to end up suffering? It is a common experience. Many of us, both men and women, start with high hopes from a young age, only to face significant disappointments as we grow older.

Perhaps you fell in love with your neighbor but never confessed your feelings because you saw them flirting with your friend. Maybe you developed feelings for a schoolteacher admired by many in the class. You might have experienced heartache if you were unexpectedly abandoned or discovered they were secretly seeing someone else. Perhaps you got married believing it would bring happiness, only to now question if you made the right choice because of many things your partner does that frustrate and annoy you. You are unsure if the problem lies with the person, with yourself, or if marriage isn't what you imagined it would be. The list of heartbreaks is endless. When "love" knocks on your door, it is sublime, but it sometimes ends in disappointment, breaking the heart and leaving deep scars.

In the beginning, everything feels wonderful. You cherish every moment with the person you love and overlook any flaws. Instead, you focus on being loved as deeply as you love them, wondering if you will measure up or if they will be equally enthusiastic about you.

Disagreements, misunderstandings, and abuse can arise. You may still be in love, but it doesn't feel the same. Out of love, you endure and hold on, hoping things will improve because your feelings remain strong. However, there may come a day when you decide you can no longer continue the relationship due to the overwhelming suffering. When it ends, you find yourself in pain, even though you knew it wasn't healthy. You wonder: what went wrong? Why did everything fall apart? The suffering is so intense that you're hesitant to risk experiencing it again. Yet, love eventually returns, and you fall in love once more, as if you'd never been hurt before.

You reassure yourself that this time will be different, that this person loves you more and does not share the same bad habits as the one before. They treat you differently, and that is why you allow yourself to hope, believing that this time you will find happiness. You convince yourself that this is true love. Once again, everything feels beautiful, and you find happiness anew. Do you remember those moments? How long did that illusion last? Was it slightly longer than the one before? I imagine that when the issues began to surface, you chose to ignore them, fearing the possibility of failure. How long did it take for you to heed that inner voice warning you that things were amiss?

That little voice nagged at you, disturbing your peace because deep down, you knew it was right. It warned you that you had made a mistake and were destined to suffer because the love you once felt was fading. It's akin to a doctor delivering a terminal diagnosis, leaving you powerless to save that love. This fear of failure makes you question whether true love exists, if it's meant for you, and if it can truly last a lifetime.

With two or three love crises, it is enough to start doubting if love is real. Does love truly exist? Those who have loved do not question its existence, but they do wonder whether it is really as they have been led to believe.

Poems and songs often depict love as eternal and all-powerful, making you believe that life isn't worth living without it. Yet, you might have found yourself saying, "But when I've loved, I've suffered a lot!" This leads to a cascade of questions: Do I have to submit to the person I love? Must I forgive everything for the sake of love? Should I stop being myself and be willing to suffer? Is what I feel truly love, or is it a form of disease, manipulation, or deception?

The problem isn't love itself. The issue lies in how love is handled and with whom you share it. A boy might be deeply in love with a girl so vain that she treats going to the movies with him as if she's doing him a favor. Similarly, a girl might be in love with a boy who would rather spend time with his friends than go dancing with her.

The examples are varied: a man might deeply love a woman who, instead of reciprocating his love, uses him for his money. Similarly, a woman might love a man who barely speaks to her when he visits.

The issue isn't that you feel love, but rather what you experience when you fall in love. The problem lies in the relationship you have with the person you love. It's the romantic relationship that falters and fades, ultimately damaging the love you feel for someone. Simply feeling love and being loved isn't enough to ensure happiness and success as a couple.

Love is neither omnipotent nor all-knowing. It is a sublime and spectacular feeling that must be nurtured within a healthy and mature relationship. Without proper care, it withers like a beautiful flower deprived of water and fertile soil. It is the romantic relationship that determines whether love endures. While the feeling of love is essential for a romantic relationship to exist, it cannot survive on that powerful emotion alone. For love to last a lifetime and for you not to suffer, the romantic relationship must also stay alive.

Being in a relationship is often more rewarding than being alone. While relationships can seem complicated and challenging, the benefits usually outweigh the efforts. For instance, men in relationships tend to enjoy better health and improved financial stability compared to when they are single. Additionally, people in relationships generally experience more frequent and satisfying sexual intimacy than those who are single.

The success of a romantic relationship largely depends on how well you choose your partner. In my experience evaluating couples in crisis and on the verge of separation, I've often found that the root of their problems lies in the initial choice of partner.

Many people begin relationships with unsuitable partners and then go to great lengths to keep the relationship alive, driven by the belief that love can transform everything. At other times, individuals may feel they are failing because they think they are incapable of functioning within a romantic relationship. They believe they don't know how to love.

Feeling love for someone doesn't necessarily mean that person is the most suitable partner for a romantic relationship. Not all attractions we feel can be defined as love, as there are different types of attraction. Given this complexity, it's unsurprising how many mistakes are made when choosing a partner for a romantic relationship.

After all, we often receive more guidance on selecting a car, a house, a piece of clothing, or a pair of shoes than on choosing the person with whom we might spend the rest of our lives. You've probably considered what attracts you to the people you connect with and may even have a mental list of characteristics your ideal partner should possess. Typically, these lists include some of the following factors:

- physical attraction
- mutual love
- they are a good person
- compatibility
- they want to be with me
- sexual compatibility
- financial stability
- intelligence
- the absence of addictions
- dancing skills

However, if I were to ask you to define each of those characteristics and explain how you assess whether a person possesses them, you would likely need to take a moment to think about it. You might respond by saying that you'll just know when the right person is in front of you. Without much thought, almost intuitively, you might feel that the person who attracts you possesses those qualities. But how do you truly know, and how will you confirm it? What if they are deceiving you into believing they have the qualities you seek, while in reality, they are quite different from what they appear to be?

Many people have discovered that the "perfect" person is not as they initially thought. Once fully immersed in a romantic relationship, they realize it was all an illusion or a facade. Conversely, how often do people reject a wonderful individual for misguided reasons, unrelated to the person's true character, only to later find that someone else recognized and appreciated their worth? Some assume that an exceptionally beautiful person must be vain, conceited, and demanding, while others believe that if someone is very attractive, they must lack intelligence. In reality, beauty does not dictate humility, and intelligence is unrelated to appearance.

Do you know what qualities your partner should have to make you happy? Are you aware of your preferences, or are you simply searching for that spark, excitement, or attraction that signals a lifelong love? Can you differentiate between love and mere attraction? How will you recognize if what you feel—or what they feel for you—is truly love? How will you determine if you have found your ideal partner?

It is important to have criteria when choosing your partner. Some are basic and essential, such as the ability to commit and fulfill commitments. Others are more related to personal preferences and specific circumstances, like the desire to have children. Beyond having criteria, you must also possess the ability to evaluate and discern among potential candidates. You should be able to accurately determine if a person possesses the qualities and meets the expectations you seek in a partner.

When you choose a person blindly, the passion often fades once you truly get to know them. Relationships are typically very loving and intense at the beginning, especially when your love is based solely on an illusion, and you don't know the person you're committing to. Unpleasant surprises can extinguish passion. However, love that is discovered with eyes wide open does not die or fade.

In this book, you will find a straightforward guide to selecting a partner. While I recommend considering these criteria, they are not a guarantee of success or happiness in love. However, they can significantly help you avoid the negative consequences of choosing blindly.

This guide will also help you avoid the decision to give up and resign yourself to a life without a partner and the hope of love, all in an effort to protect yourself. It is essential to educate yourself and prioritize the process of evaluating the person with whom you plan to establish a relationship. "Love's GPS" serves as a guide, explaining the stops and paths that can lead you to find the person you are looking for. As with any adventure, the goal is to stay on course and ensure that the process of choosing a partner does not cause you unnecessary suffering.

When I'm on the road and make a wrong turn, the calm voice of the GPS quickly says, "recalculating route," and provides new instructions. It never says, "You are hopelessly lost, you are a failure as a driver." Similarly, if you find you've made a mistake while using this "Love's GPS", pause and recalculate your route. Never give up, because even if it takes time, you can still reach your destination. No matter how much you analyze and try to guide your heart to avoid mistakes, when you fall in love, it won't be with less illusion or passion. If you choose wisely, you can sustain that illusion and passion for a long time—perhaps even a lifetime.

Chapter 1

How to Know if You Are Ready for a Romantic Relationship

When embarking on the journey of finding a partner, it's essential to begin by assessing your readiness for a relationship. Keep in mind that just as you are choosing someone, they are also evaluating you. These considerations are mutual, so I recommend starting with a self-assessment.

First and foremost, you need to be at peace with your singleness. Being without a partner is neither a tragedy nor a flaw; it's simply a status. If you find yourself anxious because you can't tolerate being alone or enjoy life independently, you may not be ready to pursue a healthy relationship.

Your partner should not be considered your "other half." This metaphor suggests that you are incomplete until you find someone who completes you. While the idea of an "other half" might make sense if the primary purpose of a relationship is to procreate and have children, it's important to recognize that a fulfilling relationship is built on two whole individuals coming together.

In today's world, a romantic relationship is not a prerequisite for having children, as adoption and artificial fertilization are viable options. You don't need a partner to become a parent. If the primary goal of a relationship is to have children, then the criteria might focus on genetics and the physical attributes you desire for your offspring, similar to how animal pairings are often selected. However, I don't recommend this approach if you also wish to build a life with your partner. Your partner should not be the one to make you feel complete or do for you what you should do for yourself. They should not be the person who compensates for your shortcomings and weaknesses. Choosing someone solely because they possess qualities you lack can lead to a dependent relationship.

A romantic relationship should be one of interdependence, where tasks are divided based on various criteria, rather than simply because you cannot perform a specific task. You shouldn't rely on someone else to do what you can do independently. This doesn't mean you can't depend on someone for help, but such dependence should be temporary while you learn to manage a particular responsibility on your own.

Your partner doesn't have to be your soulmate or mirror your personality. It's not enough to simply feel a special connection or believe that meeting them fulfills a mission. A healthy romantic relationship isn't built on the need for someone else to make you whole. If you think you can't be happy or enjoy life without a partner, you risk undermining the relationship.

Dependence suggests a lack of capability or interest in personal growth and learning. There are various forms of dependence, such as financial dependence, where someone supports you or provides the comforts and luxuries you desire. Similarly, you might rely on someone to prepare your meals because you don't know how to cook the dishes you enjoy, or you might depend on them for a sense of security and protection. These are examples of casual dependencies. However, the most challenging form of dependence in a romantic relationship is emotional dependence.

The roots of emotional dependence can be traced back to an individual's development and growth process. Human development begins with complete dependence in all areas. A baby relies entirely on others for survival, as they cannot feed or protect themselves. As children grow, their physical development is accompanied by an increasing awareness of their identity, the identity of others, and the nature of their relationships with the world.

Initially, parents play a crucial role in defining a child's identity, starting with choosing your name and making decisions intended to protect you. Ideally, as a child you encounter new experiences, and your parents guide you in developing behaviors that foster independence. Parents need to encourage their children to explore and practice independence at a level appropriate to their capabilities. The success children experience in exercising independence builds their confidence in themselves and their surroundings.

By adolescence, children should have acquired enough information and skills to manage increasingly without external assistance. They should also be able to recognize their own strengths and limitations. During this stage, adolescents often face challenges as others may question their tastes, interests, and ways of being. This period is crucial for them to define themselves and establish their own identity. Through interactions with peers, they learn behaviors beyond those taught by their family, enriching their personal development.

A young adult should have achieved a higher level of independence and have a clearer understanding of who they are and with whom they enjoy spending time. They will choose their friends and decide whom to emulate, what to reject, and what to accept. While they may still receive information and advice, they are ready to make their own decisions and take responsibility for the consequences of their mistakes.

The fear of making mistakes no longer torments or paralyzes them. These are the foundations of self-esteem, self-image, and emotional independence. If parents overprotect their children or expose them to situations without providing the necessary tools to handle them, the young person may fail and become frustrated, leading to dependence on their parents and others to navigate life.

Emotional independence is crucial for individuals to relate to others without feeling overwhelmed or oppressed. When you are emotionally independent, you can live without your partner, but you recognize that you prefer to be with them. You don't need them to live your life. Seeking a partner should be about adding experiences and sharing emotional and physical intimacy. You choose someone who enriches you and exposes you to new experiences that strengthen you and allow you to discover other aspects of life. With your partner, you can explore experiences that do not compromise your security, health, well-being, and strengths.

This doesn't mean everything will be perfect, but it suggests that the overall balance of your experience with that person is more positive than negative. Emotional dependence, however, indicates that an individual, regardless of age, still needs to acquire the necessary skills to live independently, without relying on others to make decisions, solve problems, or provide constant companionship. In educational and professional settings, the structure and guidance from teachers and bosses can serve as parental figures, enabling someone with a tendency to depend on others to achieve success and encounter minimal conflicts.

In a romantic relationship, emotional dependence can have very negative implications. It causes individuals to look to their partner for salvation. The expression "I can't live without you" reflects dependence, not love. When dependence is present, emotional stability and happiness hinge on the partner's presence and their ability to meet all your needs. If the partner is absent or if there's a fear they might leave, anxiety sets in. Not receiving a call can lead to desperation; not seeing them can make you feel overwhelmed and unable to function effectively in your work or personal life. The absence of that person can make you feel profoundly distressed.

For some, the level of dependence is so intense that simply hearing their partner's voice on an answering machine can act as a tranquilizer, providing a sense of closeness and alleviating feelings of loneliness.

If you lack emotional independence, you'll find yourself vulnerable and at a disadvantage when evaluating potential partners. The desire to be with someone might lead you to accept a person who isn't suitable for you, ultimately diminishing rather than enriching your life. Desperation to find a companion can hinder your ability to be selective, causing you to focus more on signs of interest from the other person rather than assessing their qualities. You might rush into a relationship as soon as they show interest, without taking the time to learn more about them or ask important questions, fearing disappointment or scaring them away. It's akin to grocery shopping on an empty stomach: everything seems appealing, but once you're home, you realize you've chosen items you don't like.

This dependence can also become a burden for your partner, as they may feel responsible for both your emotional well-being and their own. While it's important to derive satisfaction from making your partner happy, it's different from believing that without you, they would be unhappy and fall apart. Such dynamics create tension in the relationship, requiring constant availability and often significant personal sacrifice. By taking on the responsibility of solving all your partner's problems, you prevent them from growing and being the person they were before the relationship.

Consider the example of a woman who is overjoyed upon discovering she is pregnant. She shares the news with everyone, thrilled at the prospect of becoming a mother. However, as the pregnancy progresses, she faces various discomforts and must make lifestyle adjustments. She needs to eat healthily to protect the baby, avoid alcohol and smoking, and refrain from activities that could endanger the baby's health.

As the pregnancy advances, she finds it increasingly difficult to move as her growing belly becomes cumbersome and tiring. She wakes up at night due to the baby's movements. By the end of the pregnancy, she has undergone significant changes: she has gained weight, her features have altered, her bladder is unpredictable, and walking is a challenge. She yearns for the pregnancy to end so she can return to her former self.

While she loves her baby, she resents the loss of her previous lifestyle, everything now revolves around the child. For both mother and baby, childbirth is essential for survival; otherwise, they would consume each other. The mother would risk her life, and the baby would not thrive.

In a similar vein, emotional dependence in a relationship can lead to vulnerability to manipulation and abuse. A dependent person may go to great lengths to avoid abandonment, compromising their values and accepting unhealthy conditions. A partner might demand that you give up personal interests, friends, and family, alter your appearance, or change your values and customs. They might insist you tolerate infidelity or remain in a relationship devoid of typical couple privileges. You could find yourself in a situation where you are mistreated or even endangered.

To avoid dependence, you don't need to be perfect or capable of everything. The key is to live your life without relying on someone else to solve it for you. If you lack the financial means for certain comforts, adapt and learn to enjoy life within your means. If you can't cook, be willing to learn or make do with simple meals. Enjoy activities alone, whether it's watching a movie or inventing new pastimes. Embrace the freedom of solitude and indulge in self-care without interruption.

Furthermore, you should be comfortable with the silence of your home and the darkness of night when you go to bed, even if you're alone. If you find it difficult to be at peace when alone, it's essential to address your emotional dependence.

It's crucial not to rush or make impulsive decisions regarding something as significant as a romantic relationship. To evaluate a potential partner effectively, you must think clearly and be prepared to let go of anyone who doesn't meet your expectations.

Choosing a partner involves weighing both positive and negative aspects to reach a well-considered conclusion. A person driven by need often struggles with negotiation. By focusing on what you prefer rather than what you need, you adopt a healthier mindset. Your partner should enhance your happiness, not be the sole source of it. From this perspective, you can negotiate and evaluate based on your desires and preferences in a partner, without diminishing the importance of either party.

Both individuals should find happiness in the relationship, contribute desired elements, and enrich each other. This dynamic fosters interdependence, where neither you nor your partner feels as though your existence depends solely on the other.

If you're still suffering from a past relationship that didn't work out, you might not be ready to seek a new partner. It's important to take time to heal before entering into another relationship. Recovery involves processing and overcoming the anger, disappointment, and sadness from the previous loss. If you find yourself thinking that all men or women and relationships are disappointing, it may indicate that you haven't fully healed. It's crucial to reflect on and identify the factors that contributed to the failure of your past relationship.

Consider how both you and your partner played a role in the relationship's demise. What mistakes did you make? If there were significant conflicts, seeking professional help can be beneficial in healing those areas of weakness and accurately identifying the mistakes made.

Once you've spent time reflecting and rebuilding your life, you can begin the process of seeking a new partner, even if your official separation was recent. It's worth noting that some people remain in a relationship long after realizing it no longer works. For various reasons, they delay making or acting on the decision to end it. By the time they finally separate, they may have already been emotionally detached from their partner for quite some time.

There is no set or magical timeline for healing and being ready for a new relationship. It largely depends on how much you've managed to rebuild your life so that when you meet someone new, you're not biased or so desperate that you accept the first invitation without properly evaluating the person. It's important not to project frustrations from a previous relationship onto the person you're considering. If your thoughts are still clouded by memories of the past, you may not be ready to start anew.

Organizing your past experiences mentally is crucial. Reflect on how your relationships have been to identify any potential biases you might carry into a new relationship. This reflection can also help you recognize the qualities you tend to seek in others or those that naturally attract you. Later, I provide some questionnaires to help you document elements of your past relationships. Completing these can help you recall additional details as you answer the questions.

The first questionnaire focuses on the qualities of your relationships with close family members and friends. While they are not romantic partners, these individuals have shared special and intimate connections with you, influencing your preferences and personal qualities. It's important not to underestimate the impact of these relationships.

The second questionnaire addresses your past romantic relationships. Both questionnaires come with a guide to help you consider and analyze your experiences. There may be other elements not covered in this guide. If you identify any, seek additional information from other books or consult a professional expert in human behavior.

Questionnaires

My Family and Friends

How many people are in your family?
How many siblings do you have? _________ Ages:
What is your birth order? ___ Oldest ____ Middle ______ Youngest _______ Other
What is the status of your parents: Married__Divorced__Living together__Separated__Widowed___
How would you describe your father's personality?
How would you describe your mother's personality?
How would you describe your siblings' personalities?

Sibling 1:
Sibling 2:
Sibling 3:

How would you describe your grandparents' personalities? (if you didn't know them, describe what you've been told about them):

Paternal grandfather:
Paternal grandmother:
Maternal grandfather:
Maternal grandmother:

Describe the personalities of your best male friends:
Describe the personalities of your best female friends:
What type of people do you not get along with?
What are your best qualities?
What are your biggest flaws?

Profile of My Romantic Relationships

How many partners have you had?
How many did you choose?
How many chose you?
How long did your relationships last?
How many left you?
How many did you leave?
What were the reasons for the relationships ending?
How much time passed between each relationship?

Indicate which of the following statements describes you:
    1) When I fall in love, it is
        a. gradually
        b. love at first sight
    2) I am won over by:
        a. the details
        b. being considered
        c. the things they say
        d. how much they are like me
        e. how attractive they are
        f. having money
        g. others
    3) I am turned off by someone who is:
        a. conceited
        b. quiet
        c. unattractive
        d. passive

    e. without money

    f. short

4) I believe a courtship should last:

    a. months

    b. years

5) When I meet someone for the first time I:

    a. imagine a family with them

    b. see myself sharing/going out with them

    c. imagine sexual intimacy

6) My best quality as a partner is being:

    a. understanding

    b. attentive

    c. affectionate

    d. faithful

    e. serious

    f. cheerful

7) I know what I feel is love because:

    a. I want to spend my whole life with the person

    b. I can't find peace in their absence

    c. I only think about the person

    d. other________________________

8. What qualities have your partners evaluated as positive?

9. What complaints have your partners had about you?

10. In what areas have you improved since your first relationship?

Attributes of My Partners

List the attributes of your partners, especially those that made you fall in love.

Physical (e.g., height, skin color)	Personality (traits)	Status-(eg. social circumstances

Summary of My Relationships

Provide detailed answers for each of your relationships.

	Partner 1	Partner 2	Partner 3	Partner 4
Who made the first move?				
Your first impression of them				
What made you fall in love with this person?				

Positive attributes of the person				
Negative attributes of the person				
How long did the relationship last?				
Who ended it?				
What were the reasons for ending the relationship?				
Rate the following questions on a scale from 1 to 10, where 1 is the minimum and 10 is the maximum.				
How genuine were you in the relationship?				
How much did you stop being yourself?				
How much did you love them?				
How much did they love you?				
How much did you enjoy the sexual intimacy?				

How much did you argue?				
How good was the communication? How compatible were you?				
How much did you suffer when you separated?				

Chapter 2

A Guide for Analyzing the Questionnaires

The most insightful analysis of your answers will come from you. This process allows you to uncover significant details you may have previously overlooked. By examining your responses within the context of your relationship history, you may identify patterns, motivations, or elements that provide deeper meaning to your experiences.

Do not underestimate the value of discovering these patterns and connecting your experiences. Taking the time to reflect on your past can lead to a better understanding of yourself. Initiating change involves a journey of self-discovery. A significant part of altering aspects of yourself that you find unsatisfactory involves becoming aware of the elements that impact your life. The more you can "see" your actions and experiences, the more control you will have over your life.

Many people have shared that, at the end of a relationship, they gain clarity about who their partner truly is, recognizing both flaws and virtues. At this point, they can understand what others were warning them about their partner because they are no longer blinded by initial attraction. When attraction arises, so those the blindfold over your eyes. This "blindness" is a spontaneous reaction with many roots both at a neurological level and in experience and leaves you without clear guidance. Once you understand your tendencies in choosing partners and have clear goals and expectations, you will navigate relationships with greater awareness. You can better avoid unpleasant experiences in love when you walk with your eyes wide open and more confident of what you want.

By examining your answers carefully, you can identify what you seek and what you should avoid. Avoid judging or reproaching yourself during this analysis. Simply acknowledge your experiences. Recognizing something you hadn't noticed before can lead to greater control over who you choose to share your life with.

Consulting a professional can be beneficial in analyzing your responses. However, I will provide some ideas and key concepts to offer some perspective on your experiences. I encourage you to maintain an open and broad mindset as you explore the information presented here.

The Family Constellation

Family plays a significant role in shaping personality. Within the family, you learn how to gain attention, companionship, and love. Childhood experiences influence how you are won over by others. Factors such as family size and sibling position affect personality and influence partner selection.

Family members interact through behavior patterns and roles that become internalized personality traits. Parents not only teach desired behaviors but also model actions that you may imitate and internalize. This learning affects your perception of life and emotional responses.

Sibling rivalry, whether with same-sex or opposite-sex siblings, naturally occurs in families with multiple children and influences adult behavior. This dynamic also applies to only children exposed to cousins or other children. Attitudes, prejudices, and behaviors from sibling competition are often repeated in adulthood. For instance, reactions to family favoritism can mirror how you approach romantic competition.

If you compete for someone's affection, you may project childhood experiences of competing for parental attention. If you perceived favoritism toward a sibling, you might feel at a disadvantage in romantic pursuits, underestimating your attractiveness and prejudging others' reactions. This could lead to not pursuing someone you desire, fearing you won't be chosen.

The relationship with siblings is influenced by their number and your position among them. Parents often decide on family size and age gaps based on their preferences, not considering how birth order affects personality. Only children may be selfish and spoiled, seeking partners who pamper them. They may be drawn to affectionate individuals but are vulnerable to overlooked behaviors during dating.

Only children have less experience negotiating with peers due to the absence of siblings, limiting opportunities to practice empathy and understanding. They also miss out on guidance from older siblings, relying solely on parents or other adults for learning.

If the age gap between you and your closest sibling is seven years or more, you were likely raised similarly to an only child. However, if you were an only child but were cared for by your grandmother alongside your cousins, you might not exhibit typical only-child behaviors, as your cousins would have encouraged you to learn and practice social behaviors usually developed with siblings. As a result, you may not behave selfishly or insensitively.

The eldest sibling often assumes responsibility for others, partly due to parental encouragement. Older siblings frequently take on the role of an alternate parent, being tasked with watching over younger siblings and setting an example. They are expected to cooperate more and achieve more. When choosing partners, older siblings tend to select younger, more immature, and dependent individuals. They often enter relationships expecting to lead in decision-making and prefer a passive partner. They have little tolerance for partners who take the initiative or contradict them. Paradoxically, these individuals often resent the emotional burden of constant leadership, feeling they have no one to turn to for support. They believe they can't afford to be weak, as it would diminish their power in the relationship.

The middle child, often referred to as the "sandwich filling," tends to have a bit of everything. They compete with the eldest and aim for similar achievements while also mediating between older and younger siblings. Typically, the middle child is the most timid and reserved, opting to observe before acting. When choosing a partner, they look for traits of both the older and younger siblings, such as egocentric or very protective individuals, or someone who needs constant protection.

The youngest child is often the family favorite, more dependent and capricious, receiving supervision from everyone while others solve their problems and meet their needs. However, they might feel neglected due to a lack of resources and competition from more skilled older siblings. The youngest with abandonment issues can be as problematic as the spoiled one, choosing partners who flatter, pamper, and demand little in return.

Like Father, Like Son

The first model of a romantic relationship you observe, and experience is that of your parents, followed by relationships of close relatives like grandparents, uncles, and cousins. The family tree involves not only physical traits but also personality characteristics, behavior patterns, and relationship conflicts. Your parents learned from your grandparents, who learned from your great-grandparents. During their upbringing, they learned to perceive life in certain ways and handle it with specific strategies. The behavior of your parents and grandparents results from the verbal indoctrination and modeling they were exposed to while growing up.

Your grandparents taught your parents only what they knew. If they didn't know something existed, they couldn't teach it. Thus, your parents are products of their parents' teachings and deficiencies. Similarly, you and your siblings have inherited and learned behavior patterns and perception dynamics typical of your family. Just as genes can be dominant or recessive, family dynamics strongly influence personal development. You'll notice the influence of a specific behavior pattern when it repeats over and over. The more it repeats and manifests among family members, the stronger its influence on individual personalities.

If you observe closely, you can divide your family into different groups, such as submissive, dominant, violent, peaceful, cheerful, or depressed. You'll also notice behavior patterns related to relationship quality, duration, and interaction styles. You can identify how people handle conflicts, whether women are controlling or submissive, and if there are incidents of domestic violence, addiction, alcoholism, or infidelity.

Romantic relationships are more diverse when strong patterns don't affect experiences. When behavior patterns are evident, couples will likely exhibit similar patterns in conflicts and problem-solving. Sometimes, in trying to avoid family dynamics, people go to the opposite extreme and are entirely different. When you identify these frequently repeated patterns and traits, determine which patterns you participate in. Identify which patterns manifest in your interactions with others. If there are different family groups, determine which you belong to and identify with most. Also, examine which group your current and past partners belong to. I suggest evaluating your partner's family tree (history) to identify behavior patterns they might repeat with you if you establish a relationship.

Family is Inherited; Friends are Chosen

You are born into a family established by someone else, but friends are chosen and discarded based on who you are and how you want to live. Friendships are voluntary and free from legal commitments and conflicts. In friendships, you often find the support and understanding you didn't have in your family, and you tend to be more genuine and sincere with long-term friends. The qualities of your friends reveal your affinities and interests in intimate relationships. You share almost everything with those you choose as friends. Sex and passion aren't part of friendship, but sometimes the trust is so great that you share things you don't with your partner.

Friends can sleep together and discuss body hang-ups and sexual fears. There are friendships where you can express very intimate things you wouldn't dare tell your partner. Observe and evaluate your friends carefully. This analysis will give you insight into the type of person you get along with best. You know, there are friends and then there are friends. Some are more intimate than others. One might not have all the qualities you seek, so you complete the picture with others. Some friends are kept out of loyalty because you've known them for a long time. Others are newer, sharing professional or recreational interests. Whether new or long-standing, focus your evaluation on their personality traits and behavior. Identify their attributes and which are most desired, important, enjoyable, and indispensable to you.

Your Enemies Say a Lot About You

In addition to having friends, some will never be part of your circle because you dislike their behavior or find their actions unforgivable. It's important to identify the negative attributes of these individuals to understand their impact on you.

When analyzing your relationships, include the negative qualities of your adversaries and write down their opposites. For example, if someone you dislike is proud, then humility is likely a quality you value in others. This exercise can help you refine the list of qualities you consider ideal in a person.

Look at Yourself in the Same Mirror

Be honest and sincerely evaluate your qualities. The perspective you use to assess yourself is the same one you apply when evaluating others. If you struggle to identify your flaws or find it difficult to accept your virtues, consider what others have said about you.

In Summary...

In your analysis of romantic relationships, you may discover more than one specific pattern. Use the "Summary of Relationships" table to record the data and characteristics of your relationships. Examine this table carefully and note what stands out. Identify commonalities and recurring themes, even if they appear in slightly different forms.

For instance, if all your relationships were initiated by your partner rather than you, it might indicate that these partners lack the qualities you truly desire. You are more likely to find a partner with your preferred qualities if you take the initiative in choosing and starting the relationship.

Chapter 3

Selection Criteria

The analysis you make of your answers to the questionnaire will provide insight into your readiness for a relationship and the patterns present in your past relationships. Now, focus on the other person. Remember, the expectations you have for your partner should also apply to you. For instance, if you expect your partner to be responsible, you must be equally willing to take responsibility.

Selection criteria are elements to consider before entering a relationship. Some criteria are personal, reflecting your tastes and interests, while others are essential for maintaining a healthy, long-lasting relationship. Although some criteria may seem simple and based on common sense, their simplicity does not lessen their importance or impact on a relationship. Therefore, do not underestimate their significance when choosing a partner.

Is the Person Available?

First, determine the availability of the person you are interested in. If they are in the process of separating from a previous relationship, they may be unstable and unpredictable. People going through a separation or experiencing serious conflicts with their partner often seek out those who will listen and understand them. In such cases, the new person in their life becomes a refuge, and they may project their emotions onto them, seeking solace from their turmoil.

Typically, individuals amid a separation are not looking to establish a new relationship, as the previous one was likely draining and conflict-ridden. They may resist deep involvement, preferring a relationship that is easy and enjoyable rather than demanding. Some may reconcile with their previous partner, appreciating the "friendship" offered by the new person. They may experience ambivalence, longing for their former partner while enjoying the novelty, and lack of conflict in the new relationship.

The initial stages of a new relationship often involve physical attraction and frequent outings, which can be mistaken for love. However, it is crucial to distinguish between enjoying activities and genuinely loving the person. Over time, many people clarify their feelings and may choose to return to their previous partner. Nonetheless, some new relationships endure, especially if the individual has been emotionally detached from their previous partner for a long time.

If someone is content in their primary relationship, their emotional availability for a secondary relationship will be limited. Physical attraction may lead to a lover's relationship, but it is unlikely to replace their committed life. The primary relationship will remain their priority, leading to complications in the secondary relationship. Maintaining two relationships requires significant emotional energy, and conflicts over time and availability often arise. Consequently, secondary relationships tend to be temporary unless both parties desire limited involvement.

Lessons from Past Relationships

The history of past relationships offers valuable information when evaluating a potential partner. Understanding their relationship patterns, the types of people they have been involved with, the conflicts they faced, and the reasons for breakups is essential. This history may reveal an adult who has never had a significant romantic or friendly relationship, indicating potential difficulties in forming a healthy relationship.

If infidelity, abuse, irresponsibility, or lack of commitment were prevalent in their past relationships, these issues are likely to recur in your relationship with them. Victims of abuse may have been aware of their partner's history of violence but believed it would be different with them. However, it is unlikely that you will be the exception unless they seek professional help.

Conversely, if the person has had healthy relationships where incompatibility, lack of love, or specific circumstances led to breakups, you can expect a healthy relationship with them as well.

When individuals are stable and healthy, their past relationships often reflect a pattern of personal growth. Mistakes made in early relationships should not recur in subsequent ones, as people mature and learn from each experience. In this regard, you can benefit from the lessons your partner has gained from previous relationships.

The notion of having a partner who has never been in a relationship before is not very practical. An "inexperienced" couple is likely to face numerous challenges and crises due to their lack of experience. These rookie mistakes can lead to resentments and wounds that may be difficult to heal. Infidelity stemming from immaturity is just as painful and requires the same arduous healing process.

Even if a person grows and matures, realizing that a fleeting moment of pleasure was not worth the pain it caused their partner, the resulting distrust can be insurmountable, potentially ruining the relationship.

When examining the history of someone's past relationships, focus on identifying patterns of conflict rather than assigning blame. Many people tend to recount events from their perspective, often justifying their actions. They may not admit to infidelity without offering excuses, nor confess to violence without claiming provocation by their partner. They might not acknowledge irresponsibility, instead suggesting their partner was overly demanding or controlling. Honest discussions about such issues are more likely if they have sought help and worked on improving their weaknesses.

Typically, however, people attribute past problems to their partners. It is wise to maintain a cautious attitude. If they mention serious conflicts, remember that it takes two to sustain a conflict. If most of their relationships have been violent, there may be underlying issues with them as well. If violence occurred in only one relationship, it might have been due to the dynamics with that particular partner rather than an inherent aggression problem.

Love at First Sight: the Initial Attraction

When searching for a partner, many people have a kind of "radar" that is tuned to detect a feeling often described as "chemistry" or "the love bug" Once this "radar" is activated by a sense of attraction, it's important to look deeper into understanding who this person is that triggered it. While the attraction might lead you to believe the person is special, it doesn't necessarily correlate with their ability to love and maintain a healthy relationship.

It's possible to feel a strong attraction to dangerous situations or individuals with whom negative relationships are likely to develop. For example, individuals who grew up in a dysfunctional family environment- perhaps with a parent who was an alcoholic, addicted, or had severe emotional issues- often find themselves drawn to and forming relationships with problematic and toxic people.

Individuals who have a parent with some type of addiction often find themselves drawn to others who may also struggle with addiction. Although the specific addiction might differ, it is still an addiction.

There is a wide variety of addictions and compulsive behaviors. It could be gambling, sex, alcohol, work, and even fanaticism in sports and so on. Addictive and compulsive behaviors are usually accompanied by difficulties resolving conflicts, communicating, and dialoguing or confronting problems. Besides all the negativity with addiction behavior, if you add all these other complications, a healthy relationship is almost impossible.

"It's not just that the relationship with addiction is problematic; it also negatively impacts children and close relatives. For example, when children grow up witnessing a pattern of verbal and physical abuse between their parents, they often repeat it with their partners as adults, whether they become the abuser or allow themselves to be abused. "It's not that these individuals consciously choose abusive partners; rather, the people they are attracted to often turn out to be of that type. While they may be seeking other qualities in a partner, a pattern of abuse tends to repeat itself. If you find yourself drawn to people who ultimately harm you, or if you tend to feel attracted to those who abuse you physically and emotionally, it is advisable to seek professional help."

Let's look at an example of what has been discussed:

Sonia grew up in a home with a lot of conflict. Her father was an alcoholic who would physically abuse her mother. When Sonia tried to intervene to help her mother, she too was assaulted by her father. As an adult, Sonia fell in love with a man who initially presented himself as courteous and charming at a party. Soon after, Sonia noticed that the man had a liking for gambling and frequently visited casinos. However, she decided to downplay her concerns because, unlike her father, he remained courteous and flattering. Sonia married him, but years later she realized that her husband, although different from her father in some respects, had a gambling addiction that brought them serious financial problems and conflicts as severe as those her parents experienced as a couple.

Many people's relationship histories often mirror the dynamics they observed in their parents' homes. Despite the problematic nature of those relationships, they may choose partners who exhibit similar conflicts to those their father or mother had. While the behavior might differ slightly, the underlying conflict often remains strikingly similar. This is why we sometimes hear expressions like, 'You're just like my father; you do the same things he did to my mother. I don't want to suffer the way she did.

When a pattern is particularly pronounced and harmful, it's crucial to recognize it right away. Changing behavioral patterns demands significant effort and dedication. Merely realizing that you repeatedly make the same mistake isn't sufficient for change. If this resonates with you, seeking help is advisable. It's also common to see women, drawn to individuals who appear needy and helpless, naturally stepping into a rescuer role. Often, they encounter these individuals during times of economic, familial, emotional, or personal crisis, perceiving them as vulnerable and victimized by their circumstances. The gratitude expressed by these downtrodden individuals enhances the attraction, as they appreciate the support, time, affection, and understanding offered to them. Typically, the individual in crisis exhibits dependency traits, immaturity, and significant difficulty in problem-solving. They often portray themselves as victims of others, suggesting that a change in their circumstances would restore their happiness and functionality.

Individuals who are responsible, helpful, compassionate, and generous often find themselves drawn to dependent people, falling in love and striving to solve every problem that person has. They hold the belief that once the immediate issues are resolved, the person they've rescued will thrive and become an ideal partner. Over time, as individuals invest themselves fully in the relationship, they may begin to discover the darker aspects of their partner. They might find that their partner is always troubled by issues that remain unresolved, despite having the means to address them. Others may realize that their partner is whimsical and capricious, prone to fleeting interests, and easily discouraged.

Over time, they may come to understand that their partner often exhibits irresponsibility, selfishness, and insensitivity to their needs and interests, despite the sacrifices made for them. In contrast, when they seek support and understanding or express their own needs, they often find their partner unwilling to return the help and favors, which fosters feelings of resentment. It often takes years of enduring abuse before they accept that the person they fell in love with is hugely different from their initial impression.

If you believe that love can change everything, you are mistaken. Your support and affection will not transform a person into the ideal partner you imagine. Instead, you will exhaust yourself until you recognize the mistake. Rescuing individuals in need often fosters a dependency dynamic that resembles a parent-child relationship rather than a partnership between equals. The attraction and attachment you feel may be part of an unhealthy pattern, potentially causing significant harm if mistaken for true love. Some people are drawn to challenging individuals, viewing them as a test of their ability to attract and please. However, they often find that the relationship remains stuck in this phase, never evolving into a genuine commitment. These patterns of relationships are usually identified as codependency.

Codependency is a well-documented pattern in psychological literature, often characterized by a relationship dynamic where one person is excessively reliant on another for emotional support and validation. This can lead to an imbalance where the codependent individual may prioritize the needs of their partner over their own, often at the expense of their well-being. The partner, in turn, may be dependent and needy, drawing heavily on the codependent person's resources, both emotionally and sometimes financially. This dynamic can create a cycle where the codependent person feels needed and validated by their partner's dependence, while the partner continues to rely on them, potentially draining their happiness and resources. Literature on this topic often explores the origins of codependency, such as childhood experiences or past relationships, and offers strategies for breaking the cycle, such as setting boundaries and fostering self-awareness and self-care.

It is key to understand that attraction is simply that—an initial pull or interest. This attraction can be sparked by various stimuli: visual (physical appearance), auditory (voice), olfactory (scent), or tactile (touch). What captivates you and the triggers you associate with qualities like success, sweetness, or strength can lead to obsession. For instance, those attuned to sounds might be charmed by a deep, soothing voice, while visually oriented individuals might be drawn to striking green or blue eyes. Conversely, someone who prioritizes auditory cues might overlook physical attributes like eye color if the person's voice doesn't strike a chord with them.

Attraction can also be sparked by seduction techniques that

transform someone initially perceived as unattractive or unsuitable into an appealing figure. This transformation often involves enhancing physical attributes, using flattering language, offering thoughtful gifts, and displaying courteous behavior, making even those with noticeable flaws seem captivating. It's similar to the strategy of "putting lipstick on a pig," where superficial improvements are made to mask deeper problems. A car salesperson might attempt to sell you a freshly painted car of the model you're interested in, without disclosing that it was previously in an accident that caused significant damage to the transmission and engine. Similarly, a beautifully decorated house on the market might appear to be your dream home until you notice signs of plumbing issues. This tactic is often used to make something appear more appealing or valuable than it is, diverting attention from any significant flaws or issues.

Flirting serves as a strategy to accentuate beauty and create a romantic illusion. A skilled seducer can manipulate the attention of their admirer, disarming their judgment and weakening their willpower. This manipulation captivates the person, drawing them in with charming words and gestures. Falling into the trap of seduction doesn't imply weakness; even the strongest individuals can be swayed by flirtatious glances and compliments. This attraction doesn't mean love or kindness; it's more about the seducer's skill in charming people.

Moreover, it can reflect the longing and desperation of someone eager to fall in love, making them susceptible to even minimal seduction efforts. For these individuals, the need to feel in love is so intense that it takes little to convince them.

Attraction is the opposite of indifference. Once someone captures your interest, you no longer feel the same; you yearn to be near them, experiencing a restlessness that eliminates indifference. Many people describe attraction as a quick jolt, a sudden spark, or a flutter in their heart. Although it's often felt physically and consciously right away, attraction begins on a neurological level before becoming a conscious experience. This interest triggers a physical response, creating a pleasant sensation when thinking about or being near the person. It can also be a blend of interest and anxiety, leading to the physical changes we associate with the romantic chemistry and spark.

That chemistry and spark can develop into sexual desire, a process involving the stimulation and arousal of the reproductive system and sexual organs. Hormones play a crucial role in triggering sexual excitement, with testosterone being a key player for both men and women. Pheromones, particularly prominent when a woman is ovulating, are perceived unconsciously through smell and can heighten sexual interest in both genders. Oxytocin is a neurotransmitter released in the brain that creates feelings of pleasure and a desire to be with someone you find attractive. This attraction can lead to changes in breathing, increased skin sensitivity, and heightened senses. For men, this often results in increased blood flow leading to an erection, while women may experience heightened sensations in the vagina and clitoris, along with hardened nipples. Both genders feel a compelling urge to be closer to the object of their desire and engage in physical contact.

Sexual interest can emerge at the initial moment of attraction or develop after deeper interactions. Contrary to the belief that a friendship without initial sexual desire will never evolve into something more, desire doesn't always spark immediately. The process of arousal begins in the brain and is influenced by personal interpretations of what one observes and perceives in another.

For instance, if someone associates a particular skin color with negative traits, they may not feel physical attraction, regardless of other appealing features. Similarly, societal or personal prohibitions, such as those against relationships with married or significantly younger individuals, can initially suppress sexual attraction. However, as people grow closer and share common interests, these barriers may dissolve, allowing attraction to develop.

Consider colleagues who bond over shared work interests and enjoy each other's company during lunch. As they engage in deeper, more personal conversations, their emotional connection strengthens, potentially evolving into physical attraction if no emotional, social, or moral barriers exist.

Sexual attraction is composed of biological, psychological, and social factors, and it influences what a person finds attractive or arousing. Initial sexual attraction often involves a combination of physical appearance, pheromones, and other sensory cues that trigger a response in the brain. This response can lead to feelings of excitement or interest in another person. While physical appearance can play a significant role, other factors such as voice, scent, and even body language can also contribute to the initial attraction. Over time, emotional and intellectual connections can become more important in sustaining attraction.

This explains why what one person finds attractive, another might find unappealing. Some individuals, for instance, prefer partners who are considered 'less attractive' to minimize the risk of infidelity, while others seek out attractive partners to showcase their ability to attract beautiful partners. Therefore, the initial chemistry can be misleading and is not necessarily indicative of a healthy relationship.

You might have preferences for a partner with fair skin, blue eyes, a tall stature, an athletic build, intelligence, and a wealthy background. Yet, attributes like skin or eye color have no bearing on a person's character or their capacity to form a meaningful relationship. These preferences might be mere whims, falling into the 'it would be nice if...' category, but they shouldn't be considered essential or even important criteria for choosing a partner.

It's natural to have a list of attractions—those traits that draw you to someone, such as their gaze, voice, clothing, or fragrance. This list can be extensive, and shaped by your tastes and experiences. It's crucial to identify what immediately attracts you to others. Reflect on past attractions and note what initially caught your attention. By analyzing these attractions, you can identify common elements that define what captivates you.

While physical appearance and initial attraction don't guarantee happiness in a relationship, they don't necessarily harm it either. Consider whether your attractions are primarily visual, auditory, olfactory, or tactile. Understanding your personal preferences allows you to better assess when an attraction aligns with your needs or when it might not be in your best interest, even if it initially captivates you.

Chapter 4

Personality Traits of Your Date

Among the many attributes a person can possess, personality is one of the most crucial for the success of a relationship. Therefore, it's essential to learn how to identify a potential partner's personality. Personality encompasses the set of characteristics or traits that remain stable over time, influencing how a person behaves and reacts in various situations.

An isolated behavior doesn't constitute a personality trait. Traits are behaviors that form part of consistent patterns. If someone repeatedly exhibits a behavior or maintains the same attitude across different situations, it's likely a reflection of their personality.

Understanding how a person interacts with others, objects, and themselves is vital—not just how they behave around you, as they might be putting on a disguise to win you over. Once they've succeeded, if that behavior isn't part of their typical way of being, it will likely fade.

For instance, someone might be loving and affectionate to win your affection but later become distant in the relationship. It's common to hear someone describe their partner based on personal treatment, saying things like, 'They're attentive and affectionate.' However, just because they act this way with you doesn't mean these are characteristic personality traits. They might be temporarily adopting these behaviors to win you over.

Often, people can describe how their partner behaves with them but lack insight into their general behavior. If you're unaware of your partner's way of life, interests, and habits, you don't truly know them. If these behaviors are part of their personality, they'll exhibit them consistently with you and others. Conversely, if they're violent with others but not with you, that behavior may eventually surface in your relationship.

Personality traits and patterns are challenging to change and can only be transformed if the individual desires change and makes a concerted effort. Just being in a relationship isn't enough to change someone's personality.

In many relationships that end due to character incompatibility, those differences were often present from the start. However, the relationship continued based on the hope that love would eventually resolve these incompatibilities. The idea that 'things will change once we're together' is one of the least fulfilled promises in relationships. It is crucial to consider whether you're willing to tolerate a partner's negative traits or incompatibilities for a lifetime. On the other hand, you can be confident that the positive personality traits you identify early on will likely endure.

Some behaviors are habits and not traits. Habits resemble traits because they're repeated and often automatic, but they can be part of traits. For example, being late for appointments might stem from a personality trait like irresponsibility, disorganization, or being overly accommodating. While changing a personality trait is challenging, altering habits is more achievable, although it can require significant effort.

Habits are formed and maintained by the triggers and consequences that reinforce them. Triggers are things or situations that happen before the behavior. To break a habit, it's important to identify these triggers and try to avoid them. The outcomes that make you repeat the behavior are called reinforcers, usually because they offer some positive benefit. By changing the consequences—either by removing positive reinforcements or adding negative ones—you can effectively stop the unwanted habit. For example, if someone always throws their dirty clothes on the floor instead of using a hamper, you can change this by 1) giving them an easy-to-reach laundry basket to encourage proper use, or 2) setting a rule that clothes left on the floor won't be washed or might even be thrown away.

For an intelligent and typically organized person, simply providing a laundry basket might be enough to change their habit. However, for someone who is more disorganized, the presence of a laundry basket may not suffice. In such cases, the realization of having very few clean clothes after neglecting to use the basket for a month might be more effective.

In reality, people often take a long time to change their habits, and partners can grow weary of waiting for these changes. If a habit is particularly detrimental and the individual's motivation to change is low, it might be a valid reason to reconsider the potential partnership.

Personality traits are behavioral characteristics that should be identified and assessed carefully. If someone claims to be generous but does not demonstrate generous behavior, they may simply aspire to be generous or wish to create that impression.

It's essential to conduct your own evaluation of their personality and not attribute behaviors to them that they do not actually display. Avoid being influenced solely by their words, and don't delay the process of truly understanding who the person beside you is.

While the list of personality traits is extensive, once you've identified the ones you tend to prioritize, you can focus on those most relevant to a relationship, such as sociability, responsibility, honesty, integrity, consideration for others, discipline, aggressiveness, passivity, initiative, and empathy.

Below, we will define some traits that you can use to help you evaluate the suitability of your potential partner.

Intelligence

Intelligence alone does not guarantee the success of a romantic relationship. Unfortunately, societal biases often favor intelligent individuals while discriminating against those perceived to have lower intelligence. This can lead to unrealistic expectations based on someone's intellectual capacity.

Highly intelligent people do not always excel in their professional or personal lives. For instance, a brilliant individual might struggle with being organized, making it difficult to establish routines or manage everyday tasks like paying bills. Intelligence is not a uniform trait and can vary significantly across different areas. Someone might excel in scientific fields but have limited knowledge of literature or art.

Conversely, a very low level of intelligence can impact a relationship by limiting a person's ability to solve problems, understand social situations, or plan for the future. If you're attracted to someone with such limitations, be prepared to take on a leadership role in these areas. Differences in intellectual capacity can become detrimental if one partner feels resentment or shame.

Competition over skills and achievements can harm a relationship, as it suggests viewing the couple as two separate individuals rather than a unified entity. A truly beneficial relationship should foster cooperation, where both partners' strengths and accomplishments are celebrated and utilized for mutual benefit.

Age

Age is often a criterion when choosing a partner. There is no minimum or maximum age requirement for establishing a relationship. Chronological age doesn't necessarily define maturity or the ability to establish a healthy relationship. It's important to recognize that human development occurs in stages, each with its typical behaviors and concerns. For instance, the fear of death often becomes more pronounced after the age of 40, as mortality feels more immediate than if you are 20 years old. Thus, a younger partner might not share this concern, which can create a disconnect.

While age-related issues should be considered, they shouldn't be viewed as negative or decisive factors in forming a relationship. A significant age difference doesn't necessarily get in the way of creating a satisfying partnership; many couples with a 12-year or more age gap flourish, while those of similar ages may struggle. Someone much older than you might have traits that you find unappealing, and these traits may or may not be related to their age. The key is to recognize them as turnoffs without labeling them as simply due to old age. Don't dismiss someone solely based on age. If you find their personality, interests, and habits appealing, their age shouldn't be a barrier.

Societal opinions can be particularly harsh if you're a woman with a much younger partner, reflecting ingrained prejudices that position women as more dependent or less mature. If you're a woman, you might have internalized these notions, feeling uneasy if you're older or more mature than your partner. Have you ever considered why maturity is often expected from the other person and not from you? Why does society expect the male partner to be the older one?

Remember, age doesn't dictate maturity. Some 60-year-olds are immature, and some 20-year-olds may display remarkable maturity. Experience, or the lack thereof, doesn't necessarily determine the wisdom or the ability to navigate a relationship successfully.

Regardless of age, assessing your partner's level of independence is crucial. One significant stage in human development that impacts relationships is the transition to independence from one's family of origin. Many relationship issues stem from parental influence, **so it's essential to understand how much your partner's parents—and your own—affect decision-making, priority setting, private sharing, and problem-solving.**

Parental involvement can be beneficial, provided it doesn't hinder the couple's development or if one partner opposes it. Cultural differences can also lead to serious disagreements about parental roles. In some cultures, parents continue to make significant decisions for their married children, which is viewed positively, while in others, such involvement is seen as a sign of immaturity.

Conflicts may arise when partners have varying degrees of independence from their parents or are unaware of each other's dependency levels. For instance, a woman might feel frustrated if she discovers her husband is influenced by his mother's opinions on home decor, or if she learns that her in-laws are in the know of important decisions before she is. Similarly, a man might face issues if he accepts a job abroad, assuming his partner will be happy, only to find she is unwilling to move away from her parents.

Generally, adults living with their parents may not have fully achieved independence, though they might still make their own decisions and solve problems. It's important to evaluate your potential partner's independence before committing to a relationship. If you're comfortable with the level of parental involvement your partner allows, establishing a relationship won't be difficult. However, if you want your partner to be more independent, small and steady efforts can help, but they shouldn't require big personal changes. Visualize desired changes as long-term goals rather than immediate conditions of the relationship. If you set these expectations from the start, be consistent and firm in your stance.

Responsibility

Responsibility is another key element for a healthy, lasting relationship. The marriage vow "in good times and in bad times" and the legal contract imply a commitment. Responsibility means honoring this commitment, even when it's challenging. Marrying with a 'let's see how it goes' attitude, and considering divorce if it doesn't work out, is not only frivolous but also irresponsible.

Being responsible also means trying to solve problems, not just staying in a bad relationship. It involves making efforts to improve the relationship, even when it's not immediately gratifying. It also means maintaining fidelity, even when faced with temptation. Commitment is not about choosing the most beautiful, intelligent, or wealthy partner, but about working together to build a positive, loving relationship that fosters happiness, family, and shared goals.

This commitment requires staying true to your partner, even when someone seemingly more attractive or with a better offer comes along. While the new person might initially seem better, true responsibility lies in honoring the commitment you've already made.

For instance, fidelity is not just about loyalty to a person; it's about honoring the commitment you made, staying true to your word, and being responsible to yourself. Letting fleeting emotions dictate your actions can lead to short-lived relationships and hinder long-term goal achievement.

In a relationship, intimacy grows gradually, revealing both strengths and flaws in your partner. No one is perfect, and when imperfections cause discomfort, both partners must work together to address them. This requires effort, clear communication, and a steadfast commitment to the relationship, preventing separation from becoming an appealing escape.

Responsibility also extends to financial commitments in a shared life. An irresponsible partner can lead to financial ruin unless you shoulder the burden alone. Timely payments and resource management are hallmarks of responsibility, as is honoring commitments like meeting at agreed times and places.

If you've agreed to a date with your partner, you should keep it, even if your friends invite you to hang out at a favorite pub. A responsible person discusses and collaborates on changes in plans with others, rather than making decisions alone.

Irresponsibility breeds problems in relationships. When one partner consistently avoids responsibilities, the other may grow weary and resentful, potentially leading to a breakup. Efforts to change an irresponsible partner often require being very firm and strict, almost like a parent rather than a partner. Change is unlikely in someone who doesn't acknowledge their behavior unless their irresponsibility leads to significant consequences, prompting them to seek help. Many partners eventually grow tired of waiting for change and decide to separate.

Honesty

Honesty is vital in relationships. It means not lying to others or yourself. People often lie because they lack the courage and strength to deal with the negative consequences of their actions and mistakes. They might use 'white lies' to avoid conflicts and to create an alternate reality. A lack of honesty erodes trust, which is essential for closeness and intimacy. Trust means believing your partner won't hide important truths, even if they're unpleasant.

To avoid being lied to and encourage honesty, one must develop the emotional strength to handle the discomfort that truth can bring. This skill is often learned in childhood when parents address lies and contradictions. Punishments should be fair, and love should not be withdrawn for admitting faults. Instead, there should be a commitment to improvement.

For your partner to be honest, avoid being overly demanding or intolerant of imperfection. Remember, no one is perfect, and we all make mistakes. When mistakes happen, avoid reacting to them intensely or harshly. Overreacting to confessions can make even honest people hide their flaws. Don't prioritize your comfort so much that it discourages your partner from being honest and open.

Integrity

Integrity combines consistency and self-respect. A person of integrity keeps their promises and takes pride in their actions. They don't make promises they can't keep, they strive to do their best, and won't say 'I love you' if they don't feel it. Such individuals are uncomfortable with deceit and causing harm to others. They reflect on their actions and work to correct their flaws.

They stay faithful not because they're afraid of getting caught, but because they value their promises and are proud of being honest. They couldn't forgive themselves if they betrayed you, as their conscience wouldn't let them face you.

When evaluating a potential partner, pay attention to their values. Do they boast about evading accountability or achieving goals through dishonest means? Do they pride themselves on manipulation, or do they prefer to appear less cunning but maintain a clear conscience? If they lean towards the former, they may lack integrity.

Discipline

I am not talking about strict military order; it's about having the strengths and actions that represent being in control of what you do. It's like driving a car, where you control the direction and speed. It is you who has control of the gas pedal and the brakes. Your vehicle takes you where you want to go.

Discipline begins in childhood, with parents creating a structure and order that promotes a healthy and balanced family life. Through repeated guidance, children learn to adopt a sense of order and develop the strength to restrain or motivate themselves as needed. It is about adopting and preferring order and having the ability to control or motivate oneself when needed. Good habits reduce the need for disciplined effort because you prevent problems and difficult situations. It makes daily routines automatic and less burdensome. For example, you wake up in the morning and don't need anyone to remind you to shower or brush your teeth. Similarly, managing your anger becomes a natural part of your routine, without others having to intervene.

In relationships, discipline is crucial for harmonious living. A disciplined partner may not know all social etiquette but will adapt when guided. An undisciplined partner might resist structure, insist on their right to eat as they please, complain about commitments, or blame others for their shortcomings. They may show a willingness to improve, even if it's just to avoid upsetting you. However, you might become frustrated and feel like giving up on them when their behavior is inconsistent and resistant to change.

Evaluate how disciplined your potential partner is. Notice if they rebel against simple structures that require order. For example, do they complain about set times for arriving at places or commitments? When they don't follow through on something, do they blame others or acknowledge that they need to improve? Or do they say things like, "I don't know why they make such a fuss about submitting work on time, what's the difference if it's one day or another?"

The more undisciplined they are, the more difficulties they will have in sharing daily activities. If you are a disciplined person, you can't make up for their lack of discipline, because sooner or later you will get tired and leave them. On the other hand, if you are more disciplined than they are, and when you suggest or point out areas for improvement, they respond slowly but positively, you can trust that it won't be a major problem.

They don't have to be as disciplined as you, especially if you are very disciplined. If you are too disciplined, it could become a big problem. The important thing is that both of you can progress in this area at a reasonable pace. Not too fast, but not too slow.

Empathy

Empathy is the ability to understand how another person feels and experiences life. It's the ability to put yourself in someone else's shoes and imagine how they feel and what they are going through. This doesn't mean you think and feel the same way as they do. It is vital in relationships, especially as intimacy grows because it helps partners understand each other's vulnerabilities. Empathy is the ability to notice and recognize another person's suffering. It's the ability to understand what someone else is going through, even if it's completely different from what you would feel or experience. It requires you to be sensitive and able to pay attention to others, not just your own needs.

Some people lack this ability. An extreme example is a psychopath who feels nothing and is unaffected when inflicting physical pain on someone else. They might even kill a person as if they were breaking a chair or another piece of furniture.

Empathy becomes especially important when a relationship

involves intimacy because exposing yourself to your partner makes you emotionally vulnerable. If your partner is unable to perceive your vulnerability or understand what you are going through, they might hurt, offend, or harm you without realizing it.

The lack of empathy means that a person can see and recognize their pain but is unable to see yours. Even worse, when you point out their lack of sensitivity, they might think you're overreacting. However, if you do the same to them, they will accuse you of being insensitive and unloving. If a partner cannot perceive your emotions or dismisses your feelings, it may indicate a lack of empathy, which can be detrimental to the relationship.

Consideration for Others

Being considerate means having the ability to make others feel good by acknowledging their needs. This requires a level of maturity where one can perceive others' realities, avoid selfishness, and sometimes prioritize others' needs over their own. Consideration can range from basic to seemingly minor acts, but collectively, they significantly impact the quality of a relationship.

For instance, Pedro loves action movies and hates romance films. When he invites his girlfriend, Sara, to the movies, he always picks the film, theater, and time. At first, Sara didn't mind that he always made the choices, but after a while, she no longer saw it as a sign of Pedro's ability to have initiative in the relationship. Instead, she saw it as a lack of consideration for her. When she confronted him about his selfishness, he promised to please her. However, he never seemed to be able to go to the movies on the days and times when the films she liked were showing.

Similarly, Marcos loves how attentive his girlfriend is when he's sick. She makes him special soups, gets his medicine, rubs him with medicated cream, and especially pampers him. In return, she feels upset that when she's sick, he doesn't visit her, supposedly because he doesn't want to bother her. Even more, when she asks him to go with her to the doctor, he hesitates and argues that he has nothing to do there since he's neither a doctor nor a nurse. This lack of balance in consideration leads to resentment.

When Jorge went to fast-food restaurants with his wife and kids, he would usually sit at a table to reserve their seats. His wife would stand in line to order and pay for the food with their two children. She had to struggle to balance the food trays for the four of them. When it was time to look and find their seats and sit down, she noticed that even though he was seeing her, he never made the simple gesture of standing up so she could find him quickly. Jorge often repeated this kind of behavior with his wife. When she asked for a divorce, he admitted he was inconsiderate and promised to change. However, she didn't want to give him another chance because she was very resentful of his behavior.

Consideration for others is learned from a young age at home. Parents teach children to be considerate by making them share toys or wait their turn while attending to their siblings.

In the movie theater, they learn not to make noise so others can enjoy the film. It's in these simple everyday moments, which require adapting because others also have rights and should be considered, that one learns to be considerate of others.

When a person insists on being first, without regard for others, and isn't corrected in time, they will have trouble socializing.

In the early stages of a romantic relationship, a lack of consideration isn't very noticeable because both people want to please each other. You're so in love that you often don't realize the other person isn't pleasing you in return.

As time goes on and the relationship develops, this pattern of being inconsiderate becomes more apparent. Even though these are small details and incidents, this pattern creates a lot of resentment because it involves unfairness and unequal treatment. You start to wonder, "Why, if you love me as much as I love you, can't you please me like I please you? Why can't you consider me like I consider you? Why don't you ask for my opinion or what I want before deciding where we're going to have dinner?"

At first, what you order for dinner might seem irrelevant because the main thing is being with the person you love. But once the relationship is established, what you order or where you eat becomes important because you have clear preferences, and deciding what you eat is part of your life.

Unfortunately, over time, if incidents where you feel your partner's lack of consideration keep happening, you may resent it so much that these small issues may lead to a breakup.

You should evaluate from the beginning how much he or she considers you. Notice if they ask for your opinion or include you in decision-making. Pay attention to whether they are mindful of your well-being, no matter how simple the situation. Be alert if they do things for you without consulting or involving you in decisions that affect you.

For example, surprising you with a decision to travel to an exotic and fabulous place as a gift, without asking if you're interested in the location, if you can make arrangements at work, or if it's convenient for you. Not asking these questions puts you in a very uncomfortable position because if you refuse, you're seen as ungrateful, and if you accept, it brings complications and inconveniences that don't affect him.

If you notice that they are not being considerate of you, talk to them about it. When you confront them, carefully observe their reaction. If they apologize and you see that they try not to repeat the mistake, there's potential. Many people simply need guidance to become more considerate. However, if there's no change, it may indicate a fundamental aspect of their personality. Regardless of their other qualities, no matter how attractive they are or how much money they have, you will eventually get tired of the lack of consideration or end up very unhappy in the relationship.

Passivity and Initiative

A frequent complaint in relationships is a partner's passivity and lack of initiative or drive. This often manifests as contentment with minimal effort and a reluctance to solve problems or make decisions, whether trivial or significant.

After the initial infatuation fades, you might notice that your partner often waits for you to make decisions and tends to procrastinate, avoiding issues until they become more complicated. While they don't actively do anything wrong, their passivity leads them to do less and less over time, resulting in problems and missed opportunities due to inaction. This can create resentment in a partner who is proactive and accustomed to handling responsibilities promptly. Such a mismatch in approaches can eventually lead to a breakup.

Sociability

Human beings naturally connect with partners, family, and friends. If your partner struggles with socializing, they may avoid activities involving unfamiliar people, which can lead to them not joining you in events you enjoy. Even if they do accompany you, their negative attitude might dampen your experience. Over time, you might find yourself isolated from loved ones, attending events alone, and feeling lonely despite being in a relationship.

Your partner needs to interact comfortably with people you trust and like, and to form their own connections with them. While they don't need to be as fond of these people as you are, they should be able to engage in polite conversation if someone calls or if they're at an event without you. Good social behavior involves participating in conversations and sharing without causing issues.

Some people may have poor social habits, such as talking without listening, dominating conversations, or criticizing others. Others might boast about achievements, real or exaggerated, or act as if they know more than everyone else. Some might even share private information indiscreetly.

When considering a partner, their social skills are crucial. Love alone isn't enough; your social world matters too. If your partner is shy or inexperienced but willing to learn and improve, you likely won't face major issues. However, if they aren't willing to make an effort, you should seriously reconsider the long-term potential of the relationship.

Chapter 5

Sexuality

Gender

Gender, along with the traits typically associated with being male or female, often plays a role in partner selection. Many myths surround the characteristics attributed to gender, but traditional behaviors linked to being male or female are increasingly shared across genders. For instance, men today can be nurturing, attentive to aesthetics, and supportive without compromising their masculinity. Similarly, a woman who is assertive, career-driven, and uninterested in motherhood remains feminine.

Gender-specific traits may or may not be present in individuals, and a person doesn't have to conform to traditional roles to be a good partner. Some believe that same-sex couples might experience more compatibility, respect, and less power struggle or abuse than opposite-sex couples. It's also suggested that female couples might exhibit more fidelity and dialogue. However, these are generalizations. **Homosexual couples face conflicts and challenges in their relationship similar to those of heterosexual couples.**

Conflicts in relationships often stem from personality, past experiences, or individual skills rather than sexual orientation. If you're a lesbian, don't assume your potential partner will inherently possess traits associated with your gender. Evaluate them with the same perspicacity as a heterosexual woman would. Some women, raised with a "macho" mentality, may exhibit possessive and unequal attitudes similar to those of a traditional "macho" man. Be cautious in your choice, as you may lack the social support often available to heterosexual couples during crises.

Sexual orientation doesn't define personality or behavior. Among homosexuals, there's the same diversity of traits, personalities, and emotional challenges as in the broader population. The notion that being too selective will leave you alone is often directed at women, particularly lesbians, due to the perceived limited pool of potential partners. While it may take longer to find the right person, settling for the wrong one wastes more time.

Lesbian women and gay men sometimes tolerate negative traits, believing it's better to be with someone than alone. The scarcity of social venues to meet other lesbians or gay men, coupled with minority status and societal oppression, can foster hopelessness. The considerations for evaluating partners apply to both homosexual and heterosexual couples. The unique challenges for homosexual couples often relate to handling social rejection and internalized homophobia.

Differences in accepting one's homosexuality can significantly impact a relationship. Conflicts may arise if one partner is open about their sexual orientation while the other remains closeted, projecting a heterosexual image. Few homosexual couples share the same level of openness about their sexual preference, and these differences can affect the relationship based on the more 'out' partner's tolerance.

In heterosexual couples, the differences between men and women are numerous. It's common to hear that all men share the same flaws or that women are all alike. However, in relationships, many people mistakenly assume that their partner will think and feel the same way they do. This assumption often leads to misunderstandings, as the differences between genders can be significant. What seems obvious to you may not be what's happening in your partner's mind. The gap in perception between men and women can be so vast that stereotypes arise, with men thinking women are irrational and women believing men are unintelligent or lazy.

Do not judge a man based on how you experience things from a woman's perspective or judge a woman from a man's perspective. Avoid entering the relationship with preconceived notions. Try to understand the person from their point of view, not just yours.

Physical attraction is an essential element when considering a partner. Sexual intimacy is what sets a romantic relationship apart from other types of relationships. Without sexual intimacy, it isn't truly a romantic relationship.

On the other hand, feeling physically attracted to someone doesn't necessarily mean you'll be sexually compatible and able to fully enjoy each other as a couple. You can't assume that if everything else is going well, you'll also be happy in your sexual intimacy.

Having a strong, mutual physical attraction doesn't guarantee sexual compatibility. Sexual incompatibility is one of the most common reasons for the breakup of romantic relationships. In many cases, when couples start their relationship, they feel a lot of passion and have frequent sexual encounters, often describing this as a honeymoon phase.

When problems and conflicts arise, this sexual intimacy can be affected, leading to a decrease in passion and frequency of activity. Some couples find that, although they are compatible in many areas, they are not sexually compatible, whether due to differences in frequency (one desires more frequent intimacy than the other) or in their sexual behavior.

For example, one partner might be interested in using sex toys while the other is not. This can strain the relationship, making it tense, and often it becomes difficult to save if this incompatibility cannot be overcome.

In all areas of human interaction, we will often find extremes, including sexuality. Some people choose to live their lives without engaging in a sexual relationship. Others think that sexual relations are the most important thing and want to have them much more frequently than their partner desires.

This discrepancy creates an imbalance in daily life. Some people, due to sexual traumas, do not want to share sexually, while others are addicted to sex. Neither can sustain a healthy relationship until they overcome their internal conflicts.

Don't believe that your love and patience alone can heal these conflicts. Only intensive and consistent treatment can, over time, heal the wounds that prevent these individuals from enjoying their sexuality within healthy parameters.

What is considered "normal" in sexuality is quite relative. The term normal refers to what is common and frequent in society. The term "healthy" is also controversial because different cultures promote myths and particular ideas associated with health and the absence of disease.

Many people think that premature ejaculation refers to when a man ejaculates before his partner reaches orgasm. Similarly, if a woman takes a long time to experience an orgasm, she is labeled as "frigid." In both examples, the problem may be the sexual stimulation received from their partner and the level of comfort and acceptance of their sexuality. The issue in these cases is not physical, but rather about attitudes. Greater compatibility and connection between the two may allow both to experience sexual satisfaction.

The main complaints couples have about sexual intimacy are related to attitudes rather than physical aspects like the size of the penis or breasts, or sexual positions and techniques. Rigid, conservative, or judgmental individuals may struggle as sexual partners due to their reluctance to try new things, embarrassment, anxiety, and selfishness. Conversely, those who indulge excessively in eroticism may disrupt other areas of life, always seeking more without considering their partner's needs.

Couples typically engage in sexual activity more frequently than single individuals. Conflicts often arise when people let themselves be influenced by others' ideas and expectations, leading them to believe something is wrong with their intimacy.

Assessing someone's suitability in the sexual aspect is a more comprehensive process than just "sleeping" with them to see if they're compatible. Sexual intimacy isn't limited to or dependent on genital stimulation or penetration.

Sex and sensual experiences encompass all kinds of physical closeness, as well as the orgasmic experience. Kissing, caressing, and hugging are sexual and erotic experiences in a relationship. You can identify attitudes through the experiences you're willing to share with your partner, ensuring they align with your cultural and religious values.

You can assess their compatibility with you through kissing, caressing, hugging, and any erotic activity you allow yourself to experience. Some people think that if they enjoy their partner's kisses, they will enjoy everything else, but this isn't true. With caressing comes emotion and love, not necessarily the ability to connect with the other person.

One area alone is usually not enough to evaluate general attitudes toward sexuality, but it can be one of the indicators. For example, a person might be very affectionate, and you might wonder if they will be the same in sexual intimacy.

You can assess this area without having to engage in sexual intimacy with your partner. Pay close attention to how the attitudes I mention manifest in other moments when you interact and also when you share with other people. Remember that attitudes and traits are elements of personality that manifest in more than one area of interaction with people and tend to repeat themselves (they don't just occur in isolated incidents).

People tend to be consistent in their behavior. A person who is attentive in their interactions is generally the same in sexuality. If they aren't initially, they easily learn to be because that's their nature. A person who is generally inconsiderate will also be so in sexual intimacy.

I am aware that talking about sexuality is uncomfortable for many people. However, it's important to address it with the person you are considering. Many people enter marriage without ever having had this type of conversation. They have only dared to ask if they want to have sex and how often. Certainly, it's not a suitable topic for the first encounters, but for when there is more trust between you.

You can start with a sentence that explains how uncomfortable it is for you to talk about it, but at the same time, how important it is. For example: "I want to explore a topic with you that makes me feel embarrassed, but I'm interested in knowing your ideas and experiences.

We don't have to talk about everything today, but I do want to know you and for you to know my opinions about sex. I'd like to know if talking about this topic is also important to you."

Start with less difficult topics, like kissing and caressing. Ask them about their opinions and experiences regarding sexual intimacy. It's not easy to talk about this subject, but it's necessary to do so at some point before committing.

If the person can't talk to you about it, don't commit. That would be like buying a house without knowing if it has electricity. If they say yes, the house has electricity, but you never see even a single light bulb on, you know something is wrong and they're hiding it.

Don't get into a guessing game where they tell you that you have to figure out their preferences. Those little surprises reserved "for after we get married," tend to be more nightmares than dreams come true.

It's also not necessary to go into detail about past experiences or provide a detailed account of how previous partners were satisfied. You can ask for examples if you find you don't understand what they're explaining or if it raises doubts. You need to be discreet. Seeking the information you need is not an exercise in digging and wanting to "see" everything related to their past.

Common Complaints About Sexuality:

Consider the following frequent complaints among couples. If your partner doesn't exhibit these issues, you're likely to enjoy a fulfilling sexual relationship with them.

Haste and Impulsiveness

The average time for a sexual encounter between couples is about 10 to 15 minutes. An orgasm is an experience of intense pleasure, but it only lasts a few seconds. However, the common belief about marital intimacy is that this expression of love should be prolonged. Therefore, many people complain that their partner dedicates very little time to sexual enjoyment.

If there is no foreplay with games, caresses, and romance, the sexual experience is very short. Both women and men often feel disappointed with their partners because there is no sexual play before penetration. Spending time on romance and enjoying kisses and caresses in intimacy is one of the things frequently requested when discussing desired changes in the relationship.

Evaluate the person regarding their ability and habit of enjoying shared moments with you. Are they someone who gets distracted and leaves things unfinished? Do they quickly want to kiss you as soon as they hold your hand? Do you feel they approach you with urgency or frustration because you set a slower pace than they want? If you ask them to take things more slowly, can they understand what you're requesting? Are they able to please you?

Rigidity and Lack of Flexibility

Some people feel very uncomfortable when they don't have guidelines, rules, or routines to direct their actions. They can't be spontaneous unless they consume alcohol or another drug or are very distracted. In sex, they tend to have rules that have nothing to do with a healthy sexual experience.

They also can't accept changing beliefs based on myths, even if it's scientifically proven that they're not true. Some believe that sex should only be experienced in the bedroom and on the bed. For them, having sex anywhere else is bad or unhealthy.

Some people won't allow a kiss before getting out of bed and freshening up because they consider it unhygienic. Others only have sex if both have showered and after orgasm, they insist their partner shower immediately.

There are people so rigid that they don't allow any discussion about sexuality. Their rigidity prevents them from exploring other ways of caressing or the creativity needed to keep sex from becoming monotonous or boring. They feel intimidated if asked for a whim. They are fearful of any sexual behavior other than what they know and are accustomed to.

Rigidity in a partner is very problematic, and if you find it, you should consider the possibility of them receiving professional help to improve in that aspect. If they are a bit rigid, you can gradually explore other possibilities. Read sexual literature to educate yourselves more and discuss the information together. Practice different types of kisses and observe how comfortable you both feel with these new experiences. If your partner doesn't improve, you will have conflicts in intimacy.

Evaluate the flexibility versus rigidity of your partner. Are they someone who gets very uncomfortable if you talk about the topic of couples and differences in styles and ways of loving? Do they respond with shock, or do they calmly indicate that they know others enjoy it, but they believe it wouldn't please them? Can they tolerate you taking the initiative, or do they get so uncomfortable that it ruins the moment? Are they willing to let you take the lead at times?

Shyness

Sexual interaction requires maturity to tolerate another person seeing your nakedness and observing the expressions and gestures you make during sexual play and orgasm.

Some people are so shy that they haven't dared to look at themselves naked in a mirror, so they would feel uncomfortable with the idea of others seeing them. A very shy person may not feel comfortable. They might prefer for sexual intimacy to happen in complete darkness. Such deep shyness prevents the establishment of a trusting relationship, often leading to significant conflicts within the couple.

Observe how comfortable your partner feels when they are close to you. The first time, they might feel inhibited and uncomfortable, which is normal. However, as you spend more time together, see if they start to gain more confidence or if they remain just as shy.

Remember that extremes are a bad sign. Change should be gradual.

The more experience they have with you, the more confidence they should gain. They should start feeling more comfortable talking to you about themselves, what they like, and asking you about what you like.

There is always a certain degree of modesty when reaching intimacy for the first time. But as encounters increase, a greater degree of trust with the person is achieved, and the initial shyness is overcome.

Aggressiveness

Sex is an expression of love and the physical enjoyment of the couple. Aggression in sexual intimacy should not exist. Sexual enjoyment involves a strong and intense physical activity, where bodies move with increasing passion until reaching a climax.

The initial kisses and caresses gain more intensity and strength, to the point that from afar it might seem like they are fighting rather than making love. This strength and intensity turn into aggression when one of the two is not in sync with the other when it is an activity desired by one and not by both.

When the intensity causes physical harm to one or both, it is no longer making love but rather aggression. No matter how intense the caresses are, if they do not lead to physical harm, they are not aggressions. If both desire those caresses and are considerate of each other, the pleasure of one does not become the pain of the other, and therefore, there is no aggression.

If what your partner does causes you pain and you complain, the action should stop immediately. If it continues, even when you point it out, then you are being aggressed.

Sadomasochism is the experience of deriving pleasure from aggression and physical harm. Sometimes, it is very difficult to determine when that overly passionate sexual intimacy turns into sadomasochism. It is important to have a professional evaluation of the overall dynamics of the relationship to truly identify when things cross a healthy boundary.

A passionate kiss that hurts your lips, a tongue kiss whose passion suffocates and discomforts you, is an aggression. A bite that tears your skin and causes you pain is aggression. If you complain and it continues to aggress you, you know that when penetration occurs, it is very likely to hurt you as well. Sexual enjoyment does not require a level of intensity that compromises your physical well-being or causes you harm. If this is the type of experience you have with the person, they are not ready for a relationship.

Generally, the use of colloquial phrases and the verbalization of aggressive fantasies, such as "I'm going to devour you," and "I'm going to tear you to pieces," are benign if kept at a verbal level. However, derogatory or disrespectful comments about your sexuality, your body, or your sexual behavior do constitute aggression and should not be part of sexual intimacy with your partner.

Indifference

The absence of passion and sexual desire is a problem. It is not a healthy option to deny the existence of an element that represents one of our biological needs. When people refuse to experience and express this element in their lives, something is wrong.

Whether due to traumatic experiences in childhood or adulthood, these individuals tend to avoid sex. Some are so convincing that they make their partner feel bad for having a normal interest in sex. Others acknowledge they have a problem, but instead of seeking help, they expect their partners to understand and not demand sexual relations.

This is like buying a new television that only produces sound, not images. You take it back to the store, and they tell you to adapt, be flexible and considerate, and appreciate all the other good features of the TV.

In the end, what they are trying to say is that you shouldn't complain and should understand your partner if they don't want to have sex, which is like a TV without images or a screen. But in that case, it doesn't work as a TV, and similarly, they don't work as a partner. If they don't like kissing, hugging, or caressing, who will fulfill those needs?

Humans need physical love. You have to be honest and let them know your needs. If they are willing to change and become more affectionate, there is potential. Observe their effort and see if they do it spontaneously.

Initially, it won't be spontaneous if you ask them, and they do it to please you. If, after some time, you notice they still don't like it or enjoy it, and they don't do it more spontaneously, then they are not ready for a relationship.

Some people don't like to be demonstrative and affectionate in public with others, but if they aren't when you're alone either, the problem is different. At the very least, they should feel comfortable with a hug and a kiss on the cheek. They should greet you with a gesture of joy and show pleasure in seeing you.

People who are emotionally reserved but don't have emotional problems will gradually become more willing to be loving and affectionate unless their reserve is due to a bigger issue. Remember the saying, "Who doesn't like a sweet treat?" If you don't see any change, something is very wrong.

The Machismo Attitude

The machismo attitude shows itself in many ways, but one of the most painful is related to sexual intimacy. Studies on women's sexual satisfaction reveal that some women who have had children have never experienced orgasms with their partner.

These are often people who focus on satisfying their desires and needs without considering those of their spouse, believing that women do not need to enjoy intimacy.

Both men and women with machismo attitudes think that gender dictates what is appropriate sexual behavior and do not tolerate their partner deviating from this, as it makes them feel less of a man or woman.

This attitude usually results in the satisfaction of only one partner. The other person becomes an object for their sexual pleasure, used like any material object, without regard for their well-being.

The right to pleasure belongs to both partners, and both have the responsibility to respect and consider each other. Disregarding or denying these elements ruins the intimacy that both can share as loving adults. Even if both partners share machismo **beliefs, eventually inequality will be felt and will deteriorate the relationship**.

The Lack of Creativity

When you commit to someone for life, it usually means many sexual encounters with that same person and no one else. If you can't bring creativity and variety to that intimacy, you'll eventually get bored.

Creativity doesn't have to be exaggerated or constant. It's not about never doing things the same way or always looking for a new place to have sex. Often, it involves subtle changes in romance and foreplay.

It could be a slight deviation from the usual or special encounters on particular occasions. More than variety in positions and locations, creativity involves the willingness to play and enjoy the moment according to the occasion and mood. Explore your partner's creativity by choosing activities during dating. Observe how flexible they are and how willing they are to enjoy the moment.

Consideration in Sexual Intimacy

Couples often complain about a lack of consideration and tenderness. Women usually express feeling like they are being used as objects solely for the other person's pleasure. This complaint arises when intimacy is rough and clumsy, and does not improve even when asked to be gentler.

It also arises when the approach is driven by the other person's interest, without considering whether it is appropriate or of interest to the partner. For example, there is no consideration when, despite her being sick, tired, or not in the mood, he insists on her responding to his advances.

There is no consideration when she or he demands attention even though they are working or engaged in an activity that requires special attention or involvement with others.

It is also not considerate to monopolize the partner just because one is bored or needs something at that moment. This is a sign of selfishness and a lack of empathy. The person is unable to put themselves in their partner's shoes and consider that they also have commitments, responsibilities, and situations that will limit their ability to attend to the person whenever they desire.

Do not misinterpret this demand and imprudence as love. It is a lack of consideration for you and your right to have a life. Does your partner do things beyond simply fulfilling their needs? If the expectation is that things are done when and how they want, you will have many problems in the relationship.

Once you understand and are clear about the criteria for choosing a partner, you might ask, "And now, how do I do it, when, where?" Let's try to help you find answers to your questions.

Chapter 6

Where to Find a Partner

Traditionally, people met mainly at family or community events. These gatherings were controlled environments where single individuals could meet potential partners.

Today, encounters can happen in a variety of settings, from the most predictable to the most unexpected. You might meet someone in an elevator, crossing the street, at work, in a nightclub at a party, or even online, among many other places.

Nowadays, there are thousands of places that offer the opportunity to meet people. Some places are specifically designed for this purpose. Although there are always exceptions, generally each space creates its atmosphere, which in turn attracts a specific type of person.

You should consider what type of people, the place you're interested in visiting, attracts and decide if that's the type of person you're looking for as a partner. For example, if you're looking for an intellectual, don't search in a bar where people gather to drink alcohol to the point of unconsciousness.

To find an intellectual person, you should look in environments more suited to their style, like a library, a bookstore, or a classroom, among other places. If you're looking for someone who shares your interest in dancing, go to nightclubs or dance halls.

Using cyberspace or the Internet to meet someone has its advantages and disadvantages. The Internet gives you access to places that would be physically improbable to visit, either due to distance or lack of knowledge. You can also meet people who would otherwise be out of reach due to social circumstances.

The Internet greatly expands the possibilities of meeting different people. The main problem with the Internet as a meeting place is that it significantly increases the vulnerability to deception.

Just as people lie on a resume to be considered for a job, Internet users often lie to appear more attractive. Chatting is like a letter dialogue. It's more interactive and dynamic, but it's still a letter. If you have a camera accessory and think it protects you from deception, I'll tell you that friends sometimes pretend to be others to avoid rejection due to their appearance or age.

On the Internet, you don't have subtle information that might alert you to an attempt to manipulate you through deceit. You can't perceive if their gaze changes if they look nervous, tense, or relaxed while communicating with you.

For many people, the encounter happens casually and lightly. As communication increases, attraction develops. Many end up sharing very intimate information very early on because physical distance encourages it. By opening these doors to intimacy, expectations are created, and the illusion of a perfect romantic relationship deepens—all without ever having met in person, face to face.

When the in-person meeting finally happens, it is often full of surprises. Sometimes the surprises are pleasant, but often they are very unpleasant. What do you do when you've already committed your heart and discover the person isn't who you thought they were or who they made you believe they were?

Few people have the emotional strength to back out once they reach a certain level of intimacy and illusion. Instead of being indignant and withdrawing, they do everything possible to fix or change the situation to make the relationship work.

The most common deceptions in Internet chatting involve age, marital status, economic income, physical appearance, and romantic and sexual habits. Many unscrupulous people with serious emotional problems use the Internet to woo potential victims.

Others rely on their deceptions being forgiven by the love they manage to inspire in the naive person. Some see it as a game and, therefore, describe their fantasies rather than their realities. When they truly fall in love, they don't know how to accept and talk about their mistake for fear of being rejected.

There are websites designed to guide users in meeting new people. These sites provide questions and guidance on how to evaluate a candidate and how to approach them emotionally. They can't guarantee you won't be deceived, so you're always exposed to the risk of deception.

These websites are like cyber-sling clubs. If you're going to participate in these clubs, you should be very cautious and not get emotionally carried away without having the opportunity to meet the person in person.

Besides the meeting place, you need to consider the circumstances under which you met the person. If you meet them in a dark environment where people are barely distinguishable, in a place so noisy that you can't hear what's being said, or in the middle of an argument or drunkenness, you risk encountering unpleasant surprises later on.

There is a high chance that your initial impressions of that person might be wrong. Therefore, it's important to consider the circumstances and the place of the meeting. Compare your first impression with others you might have later in more favorable circumstances. If you meet the person under unsuitable conditions, you can try to arrange a meeting in a more appropriate situation or place.

Nowadays, it's acceptable for a woman to openly start a conversation with a stranger. If you're a woman and that's not your reality, use the means accepted in your culture to ensure you'll have another chance to get to know the person you're interested in better.

Choose a familiar place where you feel safe and at ease. If possible, select a spot where there won't be many interruptions, but that isn't isolated or too intimate. It should be a space where you can end the meeting if the person turns out to be unpleasant or not to your liking. Don't expose yourself to a difficult or dangerous situation. Ideally, find an open place with access to transportation where you can talk comfortably.

Chapter 7

How to Evaluate a Potential Partner

The process of getting someone interested in you is exciting, but it has the downside of creating an illusion that can make evaluating the potential partner more difficult.

Creating a special aura to charm and attract involves showcasing all the positives and even promising what one does not possess. People beautify themselves and strive to look attractive to catch the attention of the person they are interested in.

People tend to hide their limitations and mask their deficiencies while highlighting the positive aspects of their personality. When someone says, "I tend to be very frank, and that will always let you know what I think and feel," they often omit the offensive side of their unfiltered honesty.

Some individuals use their way of speaking to seduce. They say nice and flattering things, promising a fantasy world. In the process of seduction, they use expressions like "I love you," "I adore you," "I'm attracted to you," and "I like you" interchangeably, which do not necessarily represent genuine love or guarantee a positive relationship.

The person hearing these phrases might find it difficult to understand that they are just words and will only gain meaning when backed by loving behavior.

Generally, people interpret seductive words based on what those words mean to them. If someone says, "I love you," they think they are loved as they would love, without questioning what that phrase means to the person saying it.

Some people, with alarming ease, say loving words to others without distinguishing between "I love you," "I adore you," and "I like you." They use these phrases indiscriminately.

Non-verbal seductive behavior can also be used indiscriminately. Some people have established a pattern of seductive behavior and use the same seduction plan regardless of who interests them.

Courtesy, gifts, invitations, flowers, cards, or frequent phone calls can be part of their seduction plan and not their true nature. You will observe this behavior while the person is in seduction mode, but it may disappear once the relationship is established.

It's necessary to observe if the person behaves this way only with you, as attentive people usually exhibit this behavior with others. They may not have the same details with others as they do with you, but they should show sensitivity to the needs and interests of others. You should also evaluate if the attention decreases as the relationship stabilizes.

Some people seduce through intimidation or persistence. They say things like, "You will be mine because I always get what I want," or "I won't leave you alone until you accept me." Sometimes they can insist to such a level that the other person feels their privacy is being invaded.

Weak individuals, those who struggle to defend their privacy, or those who desire to be with someone strong to complement their weakness, may fall victim to this type of seduction. Do not agree to be with someone just because they are persistent or intimidate you. It's important to seek help if you cannot defend yourself against this kind of person.

The confidence someone shows when speaking does not mean they can truly meet your needs. Be warned that relationships that start this way often end in verbal, emotional, or physical abuse.

It's important to differentiate what is part of the seduction strategy from what is a real reflection of the person who attracts you. It's also important to break through the veil of illusion and identify reality. Discovering the truth does not necessarily mean you cannot establish a relationship with that person, but you should take other considerations into account before fully committing to that relationship.

Let's look at an example:

Ana noticed that her boyfriend often received collection letters for overdue bills. When they got married, he told her he would take responsibility for the household bills. Although she remembered the collection letters he used to get, she didn't ask or confront him to avoid problems. When collection letters started arriving at their new home, Ana regretted not addressing the issue from the start. Finally, after confronting him about his difficulty, they decided to manage the bills together so he wouldn't be solely responsible and could learn to handle them effectively.

Interviews are a useful tool for discovering what a person is really like. In the early stages of a relationship, people tend to take a passive approach to gathering information about the other person. They only consider the information the person offers, without asking or investigating further.

They don't interview the person; they simply listen. If you already know what qualities you would like your partner to have, you should ask questions related to those areas. When you converse, avoid questions that can be answered with a "yes" or "no."

Open-ended questions are more useful when you want the person to elaborate and share their opinion, revealing their true self. For example, don't ask, "I don't like inconsiderate people, do you?" Instead, ask, "What do you think about inconsiderate people?" The first question could be answered with a simple "yes" or "no," while the second invites the person to express their opinion.

Another very effective strategy when interviewing someone is to ask them to share examples of past experiences. Sometimes examples better reveal a person's true nature.

It's important to pay close attention to the stories they tell when you ask them to talk about past experiences, as people tend to avoid topics that are conflictive or make them look bad.

Don't pressure them to talk about certain topics, but take note of the issues they avoid discussing. However, you shouldn't start a relationship until you can talk about topics that are challenging for your potential partner.

You need to carefully evaluate the information you gather from these conversations and compare it with what you learn from other sources. Try to gather information from other people who know them.

If job applications require references from people who can speak about the applicant's behavior and qualities, why not do the same for something as important as an intimate relationship? It's also important not to ignore unsolicited references.

When talking to some of the people that know your suitor, consider whether their opinions are objective. Even if someone is very much in favor or against the person you're interested in, don't completely dismiss the information they provide. Try to meet close and distant friends and family, and discreetly ask them to describe the person who attracts you.

It's also important to observe the person's behavior to see if it matches their words and promises. Any discrepancy between their words and actions will be an important factor in your evaluation of them.

While it's important to see if their behavior aligns with what others have described, it's even more crucial to reach your conclusions. If their behavior contradicts their words, trust what you observe more than what you hear.

If you're unable to make a decision due to their contradictions, try to create situations that allow you to test the person. If you doubt they can live without drinking alcohol, ask them not to have even a beer for a reasonable period of time.

Don't ignore the situation if the test confirms your suspicions, and confront the person directly. Remember that a romantic relationship is too important, so take all the time you need to thoroughly evaluate the candidate.

Chapter 8

•———•◆•———•

How to Know if You Are in Love and If It's Mutual

Defining Love

Love is...

Attraction and sexual desire are not love. Love has been a very controversial concept. Defining what love is has been a challenge for poets, psychiatrists, religious figures, and psychologists. The only thing certain about love is that it is very powerful.

Love has been defined in various ways: filial, paternal, fraternal, and romantic love. Romantic love is the only one that should include the element of sexual and physical attraction; therefore, if there is no sexual attraction, there is no romantic love.

Love is a complex emotion that creates a bond and alliance with the loved one. Love, in turn, is nurtured or deteriorates based on the quality of the connection established with the person.

The depth of love and that bond depends on how well the people know each other and how much they dedicate themselves to being emotionally and physically close in intimacy.

When what you know about the person interests you, pleases you, you enjoy it and admire it, love grows. The person's skills to succeed and their ability to relate healthily with others greatly influence the feeling of love.

It is necessary to know well the person with whom you are intimately and emotionally involved. After all, you cannot love someone you do not know.

Before starting a romantic relationship, you need to determine if you are falling in love and if the person feels the same way. Although there are always exceptions, and each individual has a unique way of handling their emotions, there is a pattern often observed in people who become emotionally involved.

The first thing that happens is that the person starts to occupy your thoughts. The more interested you are in the person, the more you think about them. Then, you begin to feel their absence, so you try to spend more time with them in various activities and during more hours of the day.

This interest needs to evolve to such a level that you significantly miss the person if they are not around. It's not that you can't function, but their absence affects your mood. In other words, the person's absence no longer leaves you indifferent.

Then comes the time when you do everything possible to share and learn more about the other person. This is the phase of marathon phone calls and days spent not wanting to be apart. Then, you start sharing with people who are significant to each of you: friends, family, neighbors, and coworkers. At this point, you begin to evaluate and discuss the possibility of maintaining a serious and committed relationship.

Understanding Commitment

Marriage (or cohabitation) is one of the most important decisions in a person's life. Although the high incidence of divorces indicates that marriage is no longer guaranteed to be forever, the impact of that decision will last a lifetime.

A person who marries under the illusion of what they think is love, but later discovers that they do not truly love or love enough, suffers a terrible disillusionment. They lose faith in love and in their ability to love or be loved. Worse still, they tend to avoid future relationships for fear of suffering the same fate.

People who are abused in marriage are also marked for the rest of their lives. Women are not the only ones who suffer spousal abuse; it's just that fewer men admit to being mistreated by their partners.

In addition to physical abuse, psychological abuse occurs in relationships. In this type of relationship, the self-esteem of the abused person is trampled, insecurity is fostered, and personal growth is stifled. The impact of physical and psychological abuse is so significant that much help and personal effort will be needed to overcome it.

Several factors influence a couple going through a divorce. Much is said about the impact of divorce on children, but little about the impact of children on the divorce. A person with children who divorces is only physically separated from their partner. Even if they don't want to, they will have to continue interacting with their "ex" to discuss budget and child-rearing issues.

As you can see, the decision to marry involves an exceptional commitment. Loving a person is not the same as living with, working with, and taking on responsibilities with them. Marriage involves sacrifices and limitations. It indeed has many benefits, but you will not have the same freedoms as before.

The commitment to marry is not free from indecision. Few reach the altar completely sure. Who hasn't questioned, hours before getting married, that decision and wondered, "Will it go well? Will I regret it? Am I really in love? Will I fall in love with someone else later?"

The best way to deal with indecision and ambivalence is by having criteria that give you greater confidence in the likelihood of making the right decision. How do you know if you're ready for marriage? You should start by understanding that the following are

Reasons Not to Marry

- I can't find a way to leave them because they would suffer so much...

- Our families would be devastated if we canceled the wedding.
- I don't think I love them, but they're so good to me.
- They'll change once we're married and living together.
- They're perfect.
- Why not get married?
- I can't miss this opportunity.
- I'm pregnant.
- They insist, even when I say no.
- They'll commit suicide if I don't marry them.
- They'll kill me if I don't marry them.
- I don't know them well enough, but they treat me well.
- They're an alcoholic (or addict) but they love me.
- I desire them, and they'll be mine alone.
- They mistreat me, but I love them.

If you're thinking of getting married for any of these reasons, don't do it. These are reasons to separate or find a way to improve the relationship before getting married.

Many divorces arise from problems that existed during the dating period. You shouldn't ignore the issues experienced while dating and think they'll disappear in marriage.

Problems related to how you treat and consider each other tend to worsen after marriage. An unfaithful boyfriend will generally be an unfaithful husband.

Very few people change after getting married unless they truly accept their shortcomings and are determined to transform them.

A person with alcohol or drug problems doesn't automatically rehabilitate upon marriage. A boyfriend who physically abused you during an argument will likely hit you even more when you live under the same roof.

Despite the high incidence of divorces and all the risks that come with marriage, there are many good reasons to get married:

Good Reasons to Marry

- We can share in many areas; we are compatible.
- We respect our differences, interests, and attitudes.
- I know them well and like them as a person.
- They treat me well and are considerate.
- We sit down to talk about various topics with trust.
- When problems arise, we talk and work to solve them.
- They are not perfect, but they know their shortcomings and strive to improve.
- We are now closer and more connected than before.
- We have more good days than bad ones.
- They support and celebrate my achievements.
- I love them.

Loving someone means being responsible for the person you love. When you love, you cannot be indifferent to your partner's pain, fear, anger, and feelings. Love is allowing the other person to grow and learn from their mistakes. It's wanting to be alone sometimes but also wanting to share many other moments of your daily life with that special person. It's about desire, but also about respect.

Indeed, love alone isn't enough to be happy in marriage, but it is necessary.

If you don't love the person, don't get married.

www.ingramcontent.com/pod-product-compliance
Lightning Source LLC
Chambersburg PA
CBHW020121310726
48970CB00002B/734